How do I use

Key Words with Peter a............ ...ee
parallel series, each containin.......... All three
series are written using the s............. ntrolled
vocabulary. Readers will get the most out of **Key Words** with
Peter and Jane when they follow the books in the pattern
1a, 1b, 1c; 2a, 2b, 2c and so on.

gr.......................................ew words.

provi................................... e words, but
in a different context and with different illustrations.

• Series c
uses familiar words to teach **phonics** in a methodical way,
enabling children to read increasingly difficult words.
It also provides a link to writing.

Published by Ladybird Books Ltd
A Penguin Company
Penguin Books Ltd., 80 Strand, London WC2R 0RL, UK
Penguin Books Australia Ltd, 707 Collins Street, Melbourne, Victoria 3008, Australia
Penguin Group (NZ) 67 Apollo Drive, Rosedale, North Shore 0632, New Zealand

018

ISBN: 978-1-40930-140-0

Printed in China

Key Words

with Peter and Jane

12a   The holiday camp mystery

written by W. Murray
illustrated by J.H. Wingfield

Simon and John looked at the plans of the new holiday camp. It was being built on the island their father had bought. They were with the builder's foreman as he explained the plans to them.

"I have coloured part of the plans," he said. "The part of the camp which we have built is coloured red. The other part left white is being built now."

"Your work is very interesting," said Simon, "but it seems difficult. You have to know so much."

"Yes, it is interesting work," replied the foreman. "It doesn't seem difficult to me as I have been building for many years."

He explained more about the plans. He showed them different parts of the island holiday camp, where many people would live and enjoy themselves every summer.

John was very interested in the swimming pool. "It seems to be a large pool," he said. "It is coloured red here. Does that mean it is ready for use? I would like to be the first to dive in."

The foreman laughed. "Please don't dive in yet," he said. "There is no water in it." Then he told them that the water would be put in very soon.

The foreman took the boys round the holiday camp to show them what had been built. He also explained the work that was then being done.

They could see that hundreds of people of all ages would be able to enjoy happy holidays in the camp and on the beach nearby. They could swim in the sea or in the swimming pool, or enjoy themselves in the pleasure grounds of the camp. The boys thought of Peter and Jane when they saw the fun fair.

"Our cousins would enjoy the fun fair," said Simon. "We must ask them to come over in the holidays."

"They would like everything in the pleasure grounds," said John. "There is something here for children of all ages. I can imagine hundreds of boys and girls playing here all day long."

They walked on to see the excavators at work. They arrived just in time to see something exciting happening. A man with an excavator had just found the entrance to a tunnel.

The foreman went over to look at the tunnel. "We didn't know anything about this," he said.

"Father has never said anything about a tunnel on the island," said Simon. "I can't imagine why it was built."

The men with the excavators stopped work to look at the entrance of the tunnel. "Don't go in," said the foreman, "it may not be safe. The roof might fall in. I will examine it first."

The foreman took a torch and went into the tunnel by himself. He shone the torch around as he moved slowly along. He was most careful to examine the roof ahead of him before he walked under it. He knew that rocks could fall in the tunnel at any time.

After a few minutes the foreman stopped. When he shone the torch in front of him, the tunnel stretched ahead as far as he could see. It looked safe, but he decided to go back. He knew the others might think he was in danger.

John and Simon were glad to see the foreman come out of the tunnel. They thought that the excavator might have damaged the tunnel and made it dangerous. They knew how easily accidents could happen under the ground.

"I thought it might be dangerous in there, but it seems to be quite safe," the foreman told them.

"Then may we explore the tunnel?" John asked.

"Not yet," replied the foreman. "I must see your father first."

Simon and John were there when the foreman told their father about the tunnel which had been found on the island. The boys' father said he knew nothing about it and examined his own plan of the island to see if the tunnel had been drawn on it. Nothing was shown on the plan. "It is a mystery," said Simon. "Perhaps smugglers built it long ago."

It was decided that the foreman and some of his men should explore the tunnel, and if possible make it safe. If they could do this, then Simon and John would be allowed to go into it.

The next day the foreman took some men into the tunnel. They examined the sides and the roof as they went along. They found that the tunnel was old but strongly made. Small repairs were needed in only two places. They did these repairs and went on to find that the tunnel led to a large cave. Several other tunnels led off from this cave. They explored these other tunnels but they all seemed to have no way out.

When the men returned from the cave the foreman made a report about their work to the boys' father.

Simon and John were told by the foreman that the repairs to the tunnel had been finished and that it was safe to enter. They were allowed to go in and explore if they wished. They got ready at once and set off to explore the tunnels and cave. Both wore old clothes and carried torches.

They tried to imagine what the tunnels and cave had been used for in days gone by. "It is quite possible that smugglers used them," said Simon. John agreed. "We must search for signs," he said.

They went along the tunnel slowly, using their torches. They shone their lights all around. Now and again they stopped to listen. However, all was quiet down there.

"I thought that we might hear the excavators at work, or perhaps the sound of the sea," said Simon. "No," said John, after they had listened several times. "There is not a sound to be heard."

Soon they reached the large cave which the foreman and his men had found. They stood in the middle of it and shone their torches around.

They could see that three other tunnels led off from the cave, besides the one they had been using.

The boys stayed together to search the cave and the tunnels. They looked round the cave and then walked down the middle of one tunnel, examining the floor, walls and roof carefully by the light of their torches. The tunnel seemed to be made of rock, as was the large cave. The boys thought that both the cave and the tunnel were natural and not made by man. This was different from the tunnel by which they had entered, as only part of that was natural rock, the entrance being made of brick.

The tunnel ended suddenly with a wall of rock reaching the roof. The boys examined this and returned to the cave. They carried on their search in the third tunnel. This third tunnel was also made of natural rock with no bricks added. It did not seem that any work had been done there by man.

Once more they returned to the cave and then entered the fourth and longest tunnel. Here the roof was higher and the air seemed to be different.

Suddenly in the light of the torches they saw some steps cut into the rock face at the end of the tunnel.

"The foreman didn't tell us about any steps cut into the rock," said John. "Neither he nor his men could have seen them."

The boys went closer to examine the steps, and then started to climb them. They went higher and higher up the rock until they were close to the roof at the end of the cave. The rock face they were climbing did not reach the roof. There was a small space between the wall and the roof of the cave. Neither Simon nor John had seen this space when standing on the floor of the tunnel.

"There is room to get through the gap," said John. "I think it leads into another cave." Then he added, "It doesn't seem so dark in there and I can hear the sea. Shall we go on?"

"It looks safe enough," replied Simon. "Let's get through the gap carefully. We shall have to crawl."

They crawled slowly through the gap and then jumped down about three feet on to the rock floor of another cave. There was room to stand up and they could just see without their torches.

The cave stretched a long way before them to a low entrance where they could see daylight.

The boys were excited to find that the longest tunnel had a way out which led to another cave and the sea.

It took some time for them to walk down the long cave until they reached the entrance. This was quite wide but not high. It looked as though anyone using the entrance would have to crawl through.

They did not leave the cave at once but decided to search it first. There was more light near the entrance of the cave.

"Look at this," said Simon suddenly. "Here is a small boat." "Yes," said John, "and here is a pile of empty boxes and some rope." He sat on the pile of boxes as he watched Simon carefully examine the boat.

"What is it doing here? Why should anyone leave a boat in here?" he asked.

"I don't know," answered Simon. "I am as surprised as you are. It's a strongly made boat in good repair. I think that someone has been using it recently. The bottom feels wet. I thought that smugglers might have used the tunnels and caves in days gone by, but this boat makes me think there may be smuggling going on now."

When they had finished searching the second cave the two boys crawled out of the low entrance into the daylight. They found themselves on a flat ledge of rock a few feet wide and just above the sea. The water was washing over the edge of the rock about eight feet away from the entrance to the cave.

The boys looked round for a few minutes in surprise. Then Simon said, "We are on the other side of the island!"

"Yes," agreed John, "we must have crossed the island when we were under the ground."

"Look," said Simon, "that boat must have been pulled across this rock when it was drawn into the cave by rope. You can see the marks made recently by the bottom of the boat."

The boys sat down to talk on the flat ledge beside the water. Simon looked at his watch and said, "We don't have to worry about the water coming up any higher, as it is full tide now."

"So the tide will never reach the entrance to this cave," said John.

They did not know that a strange man was watching them from the bushes above the entrance to the cave.

As the boys talked on the flat ledge of rock they heard a noise above them. They looked up quickly and were just in time to see the face of the silent watcher before it disappeared among the bushes near the entrance to the second cave.

Simon and John jumped up at once. "Did you see that?" asked Simon. "Yes," said John, "someone was watching us."

"After him!" said Simon. He took a few steps across the flat rock and started to climb to the ground above the cave. John followed and soon they were in the woods which stretched back inland. A running figure was disappearing amongst the trees some way ahead. It was a man with black hair wearing a red shirt. He ran very fast and soon the boys had lost him.

Simon and his brother ran on until they reached the top of the wooded hill in the centre of the island. Here they stopped for a while to rest and talk.

"What do you make of that?" asked John. "Why should that man watch us and then run away?"

"I don't know," said Simon. "It is strange. Perhaps it's his boat we found in the cave."

The brothers walked down the wooded hillside from the centre of the island until they came to the holiday camp by the shore. They called on the foreman but he was very busy, so they could not tell him then about their adventure.

They took a boat to the mainland to see their father. He listened closely as they told him that the fourth tunnel led to another cave and to a way out on the other side of the island.

"That's strange," he said when they told him of the boat and the boxes in the cave. His surprise changed to alarm when he heard of the silent watcher and the chase across the island.

"I know you two can look after yourselves," their father said, "but I don't want you to get into danger. I think we'll have a talk with the police about all this."

Later on that day a policeman visited the tunnels and the caves with the boys and their father. It was decided to leave the boat where it was for the time being. The policeman asked the father of the boys, and the foreman, to report to him at once anything unusual that happened on the island.

As the weeks went by, the building of the holiday camp was finished. Nothing unusual had happened. There seemed to be no more mystery and no reason for alarm. Simon and John saw nothing of the man they had chased on the day they found the cave.

The workmen put a heavy door on the entrance to the tunnel in the holiday camp. This door was always kept locked, and the father of Simon and John had the only key.

Then the workmen left and the holiday camp staff took over. The summer came and the visitors arrived for their holidays. Soon hundreds of people were enjoying themselves in the holiday camp and on the sands.

Simon and John often visited the camp and sometimes invited Peter and Jane to come to the pleasure grounds and fun fair with them.

Peter and Jane became strong swimmers with the help of their two cousins and they learned to dive really well.

The two big boys told their young cousins about the caves and the tunnels. They also spoke about the boat they had found and the man who had watched them. They promised to show Peter and Jane the tunnels and the caves one day.

One afternoon, when Peter and Jane were at the holiday camp with their two cousins, it was announced that there was to be a Swimming Gala the following week. In it there would be swimming and diving events for children and young people. Simon and John entered their names at once.

Peter and Jane did not know if they were good enough to enter. They had not taken part in a Swimming Gala before. After talking to Simon and John they decided to put their names down for one event each.

Peter was to enter for the Junior Boys' Diving Competition and Jane for the Junior Girls' Swimming Race. They became excited about this and dived and swam every afternoon until the day of the Gala.

It was sunny on the day and many people were there to watch. The children's events came first. Jane found herself with nine other girls on the edge of the swimming pool ready to dive in for the race. She was a little frightened until the start.

Once in the water she swam as fast as she could all the way. As she climbed out of the water her name was announced as the winner.

It was soon Peter's turn to take part. Twenty boys had entered for the Junior Boys' Diving Competition and each of the twenty had to dive three times during this event. It took quite a long time. At the end Peter was placed second. He was very pleased about this.

Simon and John were strong swimmers, but so were many of the other big boys who had entered for the races. Simon came second in a long distance swim and John was third in a diving competition. Then with two of their friends they entered a relay swimming race for teams of four. Peter and Jane were delighted to see their cousins' team win this relay race.

When the Gala was over they changed their clothes and went to the nearby café for something cold to drink.

Simon asked his two cousins if they would like to camp with him and his brother on the other side of the island. "John and I have a new tent," he said, "and it is beautiful weather for sleeping out of doors. We could go next week."

"We would like that," said Jane. "I expect our parents would allow us to come."

"I'm sure they would," said Peter.

The next week the party set off to camp on the other side of the island. Jane's friend Mary was with them, so they were five in number. Peter and Jane brought their tent so that the two girls could sleep together. Peter was to share the new tent with his two cousins.

They pitched their tents a little inland, behind some trees but not too close to them. They were not far from the second cave and Simon and John soon went to visit it. Peter was busy in the new tent and the two girls wished to try their hands at cooking in the open air.

The two boys were not long in climbing down the rock to the cave entrance. They crawled into the cave and stood up to look round. The boat was still there and it did not seem to have been moved. The boxes and the rope also seemed to be in the same places. Simon felt the bottom of the boat and it was dry.

"I don't think anyone has used the boat since we were last here," said Simon.

"Perhaps we frightened that man we saw," said John. "He certainly ran away from us very quickly."

The children stayed up late on the first day of their camping holiday. They did not get their beds ready until the sun went down. Then Peter, Jane and Mary prepared for sleep.

Simon and John wanted to go out to look at the stars as they had been reading a book about the night sky. They explained to Peter that they would be very close to the tents and that they would be away only a few minutes. They took their book, a torch and a pair of binoculars.

The two brothers lay down in the grass on the top of a small cliff. From where they lay they could see the water below, and the entrance to the cave they had found.

Simon turned his binoculars towards the stars. John got his torch ready to look at his book. He was just going to turn it on when he stopped and touched Simon's arm. He spoke very quietly. "Look, Simon. Look out to sea. What is that flashing light?"

Simon turned the binoculars out to sea. "Where?" he asked. Then he said, "I can see the flashing light now. It is coming from a ship a long way out."

As they lay on the cliff top Simon and John felt excited. They thought that the flashing light from the mysterious ship could be a signal to someone on the shore. They began to think of smugglers.

Then the flashing light stopped. Suddenly they heard a slight noise below them and their eyes turned towards the cave entrance by the water's edge. There they saw a figure moving on the ledge of rock outside the cave. After a few minutes they could make out what was happening. A man was quietly pushing a boat on to the water. He climbed in, turned the boat out to sea and began to row.

As the man rowed the boat he faced the shore. Simon and John kept their heads well down in the grass so that they would not be seen.

When the man was out of sight, Simon spoke. "I think that was the man in the red shirt we saw running away from the cave the other day," he said.

"I believe that he is going out to that ship and that the flashing light was a signal to him," said John.

"Yes," replied Simon. "It looks very mysterious. He may be a smuggler."

The two brothers decided that John should go back to the tents and wait there with the others, while Simon stayed to keep watch on the cliff top. They did not want the younger children to become frightened.

It was a long time before the small boat appeared again. The same man was rowing as the boat moved slowly and quietly towards the rock ledge by the cave entrance. There was only a slight noise as the boat was pulled into the cave. Before it went out of sight, Simon's sharp eyes had seen some boxes in it.

The man did not come out of the cave again, so Simon returned to where the tents were pitched. John was still awake, and he and Simon talked for some time before they went to sleep. They believed that the man they had seen had returned to the other side of the island through the caves and tunnels. This meant that he had somehow or other got a key to the tunnel door, as this was always kept locked.

In the morning they moved their tents to another part of the island before Simon set off to report to his father and the police.

Simon returned to the island with two policemen. They were not in uniform as they thought it better not to wear uniform when making enquiries in the holiday camp. First they saw the manager of the camp to tell him what had happened. He said that he did not know the man they wanted, although he might be working in the camp. Many men worked there during the summer and he could not get to know them all.

It was decided that one of the policemen would watch the tunnel door. The other would go with Simon to the other side of the island to watch the entrance to the cave.

Simon, and the policeman with him, went round the island in a small motor boat. They stopped the boat where they could watch the cave entrance without themselves being seen.

John stayed with Peter and the two girls at their own little camp until the afternoon. Then the parents of Peter and Jane arrived. They had come to see the holiday camp for the first time, and the manager had told them of the enquiry going on. They thought it best to take the young children home that evening.

Peter and the two girls did not like being taken home while something exciting was going on. However, their parents promised them that they could go camping again soon.

John went to the camp manager to find out what was happening. Then he took turns with the policeman who was on duty watching the tunnel door.

When darkness came, Simon and the other policeman decided to enter the cave. They did so very quietly and then examined the smuggler's boat. To their surprise it was empty. They had expected to find in the boat the boxes Simon had seen the night before.

Making as little noise as possible, they walked through the cave towards the gap which joined it to the tunnel. As they went they searched the cave for the missing boxes, but with no result.

They crawled through the gap and continued their search, this time in the tunnel. "Still no luck," said the policeman to Simon, speaking very quietly. "No," replied Simon, "we must look round the big cave now."

However, they had no better luck in that cave. This left the other three tunnels. In the one that led to the holiday camp they came across a pile of boxes.

The policeman opened some of the boxes to examine the contents. By their torchlight they could see watches, cameras, jewellery and some small and large bottles.

The policeman wrote in his notebook for several minutes. Then, putting his notebook away, he said to Simon, "The contents of these boxes are all smuggled goods, without a doubt. The customs duty on all these goods is high. The smugglers meant to sell without paying any customs duty. Now all we have to do is to catch the smugglers."

As he was speaking, the policeman put the tops back on the boxes. Then he sat down on one of the boxes. "If we sit here long enough there's no doubt that they will come to collect the goods," he said.

They prepared themselves for a long wait in the darkness. They knew it might be difficult to keep awake for a very long time.

After a while the policeman said, "We'll share the time in keeping watch. You go to sleep if you can, while I keep a sharp look-out. I can rest later."

Simon agreed. He tried to go to sleep but he couldn't do so. He felt that at any minute something exciting might happen.

It was very quiet in the tunnel. The policeman and Simon felt sure that they would hear if anyone opened the tunnel door. This door was about twenty yards away from where they were sitting.

It was early morning when they suddenly heard a click. This was followed by the sound of the door opening. Then there was another click as the door shut. Someone had come into the tunnel.

Simon and the policeman stood up. They could see a moving light a few yards away. It was coming quickly towards them. Then several things happened at the same time. The policeman turned on his torch, someone else opened the tunnel door and ran towards them, and a man started shouting.

Lights were flashing and men were running. Simon caught hold of the man he thought was the smuggler and they both fell down. Two more figures fell over them as they were on the floor.

Then Simon found that he had caught hold of a policeman, and that his brother John and the other policeman were on the ground with them.

Somehow the smuggler had got free and was running quickly through the large cave towards the sea.

"After him!" shouted the policemen.

Simon and John joined the two policemen in the chase through the cave. The smuggler was some yards ahead at the start and he ran very fast. He ran straight through the big cave, along the fourth tunnel and quickly climbed the steps in the rock towards the gap above.

As he crawled through the gap one of the policemen saw him in the light of his torch. "There he goes!" he called. "He can't get away!"

But the smuggler was still well in the lead as he raced through the second cave. He quickly moved on all fours through the cave entrance out on to the rock ledge.

By the ledge he saw the small motor boat which had been used by Simon and one of the policemen. Jumping in, he pushed off and attempted to start the motor. He failed in his first attempt to get the engine going. As the policeman and the brothers came on to the rock ledge they saw the man in the boat about ten yards out.

The smuggler again tried to start the motor but again he failed. Then both the policemen dived into the water to get to the boat. They were both good swimmers.

The smuggler saw the two policemen dive into the water and start to swim towards him. He stood up in the boat and dived out of it, away from the two men who were quickly coming close to him.

The smuggler was also a strong swimmer. He headed out to sea towards the ship which could just be seen in the distance.

One of the policemen swam after him. The other climbed into the boat and after a few minutes started the engine. He then followed the swimmers in the boat. When he came to the second policeman he stopped the boat to let him climb in. Then they headed for the smuggler, who was still in the water.

They soon caught up with the smuggler, who then gave in. "All right," he said, "I give up." He then climbed into the boat.

Simon and John had watched the end of the chase from the rock ledge outside the cave.

As they saw the smuggler get into the boat Simon said, "Well, that is the end of the mystery at the holiday camp."

"What a story to tell Peter and Jane," said John.

New words used in this book

Total number of new words: 126